Gröls Verlage

„Bücher sind wie Fallschirme. Sie nützen uns nichts, wenn wir sie nicht öffnen."

**Gröls Verlag**

## Redaktionelle Hinweise und Impressum

Das vorliegende Werk wurde zugunsten der Authentizität sehr zurückhaltend bearbeitet. So wurden etwa ursprüngliche Rechtschreibfehler *nicht* systematisch behoben, denn kleine Unvollkommenheiten machen das Buch – wie im Übrigen den Menschen – erst authentisch. Mitunter wurden jedoch zum Beispiel Absätze behutsam neu getrennt, um den Lesefluss zu erleichtern.

Um die Texte zu rekonstruieren, werden antiquarische Bücher von Lesegeräten gescannt und dann durch eine Software lesbar gemacht. Der so entstandene Text wird von Menschen gegengelesen und korrigiert – hierbei treten auch Fehler auf. Wenn Sie ebenfalls antiquarische Texte einreichen möchten, finden Sie weitere Informationen auf www.groels.de

Viel Freude bei der Lektüre wünscht Ihnen das Team des Gröls-Verlags.

## Adressen

Verleger: Sophia Gröls, Im Borngrund 26, 61440 Oberursel

Externer Dienstleister für Distribution & Herstellung: BoD, In de Tarpen 42, 22848 Norderstedt

**Unsere „Edition | Werke der Weltliteratur"** hat den Anspruch, eine der größten und vollständigsten Sammlungen klassischer Literatur in deutscher Sprache zu sein. Nach und nach versammeln wir hier nicht nur die „üblichen Verdächtigen" von Goethe bis Schiller, sondern auch Kleinode der vergangenen Jahrhunderte, die – zu Unrecht – drohen, in Vergessenheit zu geraten. Wir kultivieren und kuratieren damit einen der wertvollsten Bereiche der abendländischen Kultur. Kleine Auswahl:

**Francis Bacon** • Neues Organon • **Balzac** • Glanz und Elend der Kurtisanen • **Joachim H. Campe** • Robinson der Jüngere • **Dante Alighieri** • Die Göttliche Komödie • **Daniel Defoe** • Robinson Crusoe • **Charles Dickens** • Oliver Twist • **Denis Diderot** • Jacques der Fatalist • **Fjodor Dostojewski** • Schuld und Sühne • **Arthur Conan Doyle** • Der Hund von Baskerville • **Marie von Ebner-Eschenbach** • Das Gemeindekind • **Elisabeth von Österreich** • Das Poetische Tagebuch • **Friedrich Engels** • Die Lage der arbeitenden Klasse • **Ludwig Feuerbach** • Das Wesen des Christentums • **Johann G. Fichte** • Reden an die deutsche Nation • **Fitzgerald** • Zärtlich ist die Nacht • **Flaubert** • Madame Bovary • **Gorch Fock** • Seefahrt ist not! • **Theodor Fontane** • Effi Briest • **Robert Musil** • Über die Dummheit • **Edgar Wallace** • Der Frosch mit der Maske • **Jakob Wassermann** • Der Fall Maurizius • **Oscar Wilde** • Das Bildnis des Dorian Grey • **Émile Zola** • Germinal • **Stefan Zweig** • Schachnovelle • **Hugo von Hofmannsthal** • Der Tor und der Tod • **Anton Tschechow** • Ein Heiratsantrag • **Arthur Schnitzler** • Reigen • **Friedrich Schiller** • Kabale und Liebe • **Nicolo Machiavelli** • Der Fürst • **Gotthold E. Lessing** • Nathan der Weise • **Augustinus** • Die Bekenntnisse des heiligen Augustinus • **Marcus Aurelius** • Selbstbetrachtungen • **Charles Baudelaire** • Die Blumen des Bösen • **Harriett Stowe** • Onkel Toms Hütte • **Walter Benjamin** • Deutsche Menschen • **Hugo Bettauer** • Die Stadt ohne Juden • **Lewis Caroll** • *und viele mehr….*

# William Blake

# Songs of Innocence

# And

# Songs of Experience

## Inhalt

# Songs of Innocence

## INTRODUCTION

Piping down the valleys wild,

Piping songs of pleasant glee,

On a cloud I saw a child,

And he laughing said to me:

'Pipe a song about a Lamb!'

So I piped with merry cheer.

'Piper, pipe that song again.'

So I piped: he wept to hear.

'Drop thy pipe, thy happy pipe;

Sing thy songs of happy cheer!'

So I sung the same again,

While he wept with joy to hear.

'Piper, sit thee down and write

In a book, that all may read.'

So he vanished from my sight;

And I plucked a hollow reed,

And I made a rural pen,

And I stained the water clear,

And I wrote my happy songs

Every child may joy to hear.

## THE SHEPHERD

How sweet is the shepherd's sweet lot!

From the morn to the evening he strays;

He shall follow his sheep all the day,

And his tongue shall be fillèd with praise.

For he hears the lambs' innocent call,

And he hears the ewes' tender reply;

He is watchful while they are in peace,

For they know when their shepherd is nigh.

## THE ECHOING GREEN

The sun does arise,

And make happy the skies;

The merry bells ring

To welcome the Spring;

The skylark and thrush,

The birds of the bush,

Sing louder around

To the bells' cheerful sound;

While our sports shall be seen

On the echoing green.

Old John, with white hair,

Does laugh away care,

Sitting under the oak,

Among the old folk.

They laugh at our play,

And soon they all say,

'Such, such were the joys

When we all—girls and boys—

In our youth-time were seen

On the echoing green.'

Till the little ones, weary,

No more can be merry:

The sun does descend,

And our sports have an end.

Round the laps of their mothers

Many sisters and brothers,

Like birds in their nest,

Are ready for rest,

And sport no more seen

On the darkening green.

## THE LAMB

Little lamb, who made thee?

Does thou know who made thee,

Gave thee life, and bid thee feed

By the stream and o'er the mead;

Gave thee clothing of delight,

Softest clothing, woolly, bright;

Gave thee such a tender voice,

Making all the vales rejoice?

Little lamb, who made thee?

Does thou know who made thee?

Little lamb, I'll tell thee;

Little lamb, I'll tell thee:

He is callèd by thy name,

For He calls Himself a Lamb.

He is meek, and He is mild,

He became a little child.

I a child, and thou a lamb,

We are callèd by His name.

Little lamb, God bless thee!

Little lamb, God bless thee!

## THE LITTLE BLACK BOY

My mother bore me in the southern wild,

And I am black, but O my soul is white!

White as an angel is the English child,

But I am black, as if bereaved of light.

My mother taught me underneath a tree,

And, sitting down before the heat of day,

She took me on her lap and kissèd me,

And, pointing to the East, began to say:

'Look on the rising sun: there God does live,

And gives His light, and gives His heat away,

And flowers and trees and beasts and men receive

Comfort in morning, joy in the noonday.

'And we are put on earth a little space,

That we may learn to bear the beams of love;

And these black bodies and this sunburnt face

Are but a cloud, and like a shady grove.

‘For, when our souls have learned the heat to bear,

The cloud will vanish, we shall hear His voice,

Saying, “Come out from the grove, my love and care,

And round my golden tent like lambs rejoice.”’

Thus did my mother say, and kissed me,

And thus I say to little English boy.

When I from black, and he from white cloud free,

And round the tent of God like lambs we joy,

I’ll shade him from the heat till he can bear

To lean in joy upon our Father’s knee;

And then I'll stand and stroke his silver hair,

And be like him, and he will then love me.

## THE BLOSSOM

Merry, merry sparrow!

Under leaves so green

A happy blossom

Sees you, swift as arrow,

Seek your cradle narrow,

Near my bosom.

Pretty, pretty robin!

Under leaves so green

A happy blossom

Hears you sobbing, sobbing,

Pretty, pretty robin,

Near my bosom.

## THE CHIMNEY-SWEEPER

When my mother died I was very young,

And my father sold me while yet my tongue

Could scarcely cry 'Weep! weep! weep! weep!'

So your chimneys I sweep, and in soot I sleep.

There's little Tom Dacre, who cried when his head,
That curled like a lamb's back, was shaved; so I said,
'Hush, Tom! never mind it, for, when your head's bare,
You know that the soot cannot spoil your white hair.'

And so he was quiet, and that very night,
As Tom was a-sleeping, he had such a sight!—
That thousands of sweepers, Dick, Joe, Ned, and Jack,
Were all of them locked up in coffins of black.

And by came an angel, who had a bright key,
And he opened the coffins, and set them all free;

Then down a green plain, leaping, laughing, they run
And wash in a river, and shine in the sun.
Then naked and white, all their bags left behind,
They rise upon clouds, and sport in the wind:
And the angel told Tom, if he'd be a good boy,
He'd have God for his father, and never want joy.
And so Tom awoke, and we rose in the dark,
And got with our bags and our brushes to work.
Though the morning was cold, Tom was happy and warm:
So, if all do their duty, they need not fear harm.

## THE LITTLE BOY LOST

'Father, father, where are you going?

O do not walk so fast!

Speak, father, speak to your little boy,

Or else I shall be lost.'

The night was dark, no father was there,

The child was wet with dew;

The mire was deep, and the child did weep,

And away the vapour flew.

## THE LITTLE BOY FOUND

The little boy lost in the lonely fen,

Led by the wandering light,

Began to cry, but God, ever nigh,

Appeared like his father, in white.

He kissed the child, and by the hand led,

And to his mother brought,

Who in sorrow pale, through the lonely dale,

Her little boy weeping sought.

## LAUGHING SONG

When the green woods laugh with the voice of joy,

And the dimpling stream runs laughing by;

When the air does laugh with our merry wit,

And the green hill laughs with the noise of it;

When the meadows laugh with lively green,

And the grasshopper laughs in the merry scene;

When Mary and Susan and Emily

With their sweet round mouths sing 'Ha ha he!'

When the painted birds laugh in the shade,

Where our table with cherries and nuts is spread:

Come live, and be merry, and join with me,

To sing the sweet chorus of 'Ha ha he!'

## A CRADLE SONG

Sweet dreams, form a shade

O'er my lovely infant's head!

Sweet dreams of pleasant streams

By happy, silent, moony beams!

Sweet Sleep, with soft down

Weave thy brows an infant crown!

Sweet Sleep, angel mild,

Hover o'er my happy child!

Sweet smiles, in the night

Hover over my delight!

Sweet smiles, mother's smiles,

All the livelong night beguiles.

Sweet moans, dovelike sighs,

Chase not slumber from thy eyes!

Sweet moans, sweeter smiles,

All the dovelike moans beguiles.

Sleep, sleep, happy child!

All creation slept and smiled.

Sleep, sleep, happy sleep,

While o'er thee thy mother weep.

Sweet babe, in thy face

Holy image I can trace;

Sweet babe, once like thee

Thy Maker lay, and wept for me:

Wept for me, for thee, for all,

When He was an infant small.

Thou His image ever see,

Heavenly face that smiles on thee!

Smiles on thee, on me, on all,

Who became an infant small;

Infant smiles are His own smiles;

Heaven and earth to peace beguiles.

## THE DIVINE IMAGE

To Mercy, Pity, Peace, and Love,

All pray in their distress,

And to these virtues of delight

Return their thankfulness.

For Mercy, Pity, Peace, and Love,

Is God our Father dear;

And Mercy, Pity, Peace, and Love,

Is man, His child and care.

For Mercy has a human heart;

Pity, a human face;

And Love, the human form divine:

And Peace the human dress.

Then every man, of every clime,

That prays in his distress,

Prays to the human form divine:

Love, Mercy, Pity, Peace.

And all must love the human form,

In heathen, Turk, or Jew.

Where Mercy, Love, and Pity dwell,

There God is dwelling too.

## HOLY THURSDAY

'Twas on a holy Thursday, their innocent faces clean,

The children walking two and two, in red, and blue, and green:

Grey-headed beadles walked before, with wands as white as snow,

Till into the high dome of Paul's they like Thames waters flow.

O what a multitude they seemed, these flowers of London town!

Seated in companies they sit, with radiance all their own.

The hum of multitudes was there, but multitudes of lambs,

Thousands of little boys and girls raising their innocent hands.

Now like a mighty wind they raise to heaven the voice of song,

Or like harmonious thunderings the seats of heaven among:

Beneath them sit the aged men, wise guardians of the poor.

Then cherish pity, lest you drive an angel from your door.

## NIGHT

The sun descending in the West,

The evening star does shine;

The birds are silent in their nest,

And I must seek for mine.

The moon, like a flower

In heaven's high bower,

With silent delight,

Sits and smiles on the night.

Farewell, green fields and happy groves,

Where flocks have took delight,

Where lambs have nibbled, silent moves

The feet of angels bright;

Unseen, they pour blessing,

And joy without ceasing,

On each bud and blossom,

And each sleeping bosom.

They look in every thoughtless nest
Where birds are covered warm;
They visit caves of every beast,
To keep them all from harm:
If they see any weeping
That should have been sleeping,
They pour sleep on their head,
And sit down by their bed.

When wolves and tigers howl for prey,
They pitying stand and weep;
Seeking to drive their thirst away,

And keep them from the sheep.

But, if they rush dreadful,

The angels, most heedful,

Receive each mild spirit,

New worlds to inherit.

And there the lion's ruddy eyes

Shall flow with tears of gold:

And pitying the tender cries,

And walking round the fold:

Saying: 'Wrath by His meekness,

And, by His health, sickness,

Is driven away

From our immortal day.

'And now beside thee, bleating lamb,

I can lie down and sleep,

Or think on Him who bore thy name,

Graze after thee, and weep.

For, washed in life's river,

My bright mane for ever

Shall shine like the gold,

As I guard o'er the fold.'

## SPRING

Sound the flute!

Now it’s mute!

Birds delight,

Day and night,

Nightingale,

In the dale,

Lark in sky,—

Merrily,

Merrily, merrily to welcome in the year.

Little boy,

Full of joy;

Little girl,

Sweet and small;

Cock does crow,

So do you;

Merry voice,

Infant noise;

Merrily, merrily to welcome in the year.

Little lamb,

Here I am;

Come and lick

My white neck;

Let me pull

Your soft wool;

Let me kiss

Your soft face;

Merrily, merrily we welcome in the year.

## NURSE'S SONG

When voices of children are heard on the green,

And laughing is heard on the hill,

My heart is at rest within my breast,

  And everything else is still.

'Then come home, my children, the sun is gone down,

  And the dews of night arise;

Come, come, leave off play, and let us away,

  Till the morning appears in the skies.'

'No, no, let us play, for it is yet day,

  And we cannot go to sleep;

Besides, in the sky the little birds fly,

  And the hills are all covered with sheep.'

'Well, well, go and play till the light fades away,

And then go home to bed.'

The little ones leaped, and shouted, and laughed,

And all the hills echoèd.

## INFANT JOY

'I have no name;

I am but two days old.'

What shall I call thee?

'I happy am,

Joy is my name.'

Sweet joy befall thee!

Pretty joy!

Sweet joy, but two days old.

Sweet joy I call thee:

Thou dost smile,

I sing the while;

Sweet joy befall thee!

## A DREAM

Once a dream did weave a shade

O'er my angel-guarded bed,

That an emmet lost its way
Where on grass methought I lay.

Troubled, wildered, and forlorn,
Dark, benighted, travel-worn,
Over many a tangled spray,
All heart-broke, I heard her say:

'O my children! do they cry,
Do they hear their father sigh?
Now they look abroad to see,
Now return and weep for me.'

Pitying, I dropped a tear:

But I saw a glow-worm near,

Who replied, ‘What wailing wight

Calls the watchman of the night?’

‘I am set to light the ground,

While the beetle goes his round:

Follow now the beetle’s hum;

Little wanderer, hie thee home!’

## ON ANOTHER'S SORROW

Can I see another's woe,

And not be in sorrow too?

Can I see another's grief,

And not seek for kind relief?

Can I see a falling tear,

And not feel my sorrow's share?

Can a father see his child

Weep, nor be with sorrow filled?

Can a mother sit and hear

An infant groan, an infant fear?

No, no! never can it be!

Never, never can it be!

And can He who smiles on all

Hear the wren with sorrows small,

Hear the small bird's grief and care,

Hear the woes that infants bear—

And not sit beside the nest,

Pouring pity in their breast,

And not sit the cradle near,

Weeping tear on infant's tear?

And not sit both night and day,

Wiping all our tears away?

O no! never can it be!

Never, never can it be!

He doth give His joy to all:

He becomes an infant small,

He becomes a man of woe,

He doth feel the sorrow too.

Think not thou canst sigh a sigh,

And thy Maker is not by:

Think not thou canst weep a tear,

And thy Maker is not near.

O He gives to us His joy,

That our grief He may destroy:

Till our grief is fled and gone

He doth sit by us and moan.

## SONGS OF EXPERIENCE

### INTRODUCTION

Hear the voice of the Bard,

Who present, past, and future, sees;

Whose ears have heard

The Holy Word

That walked among the ancient trees;

Calling the lapséd soul,

And weeping in the evening dew;

That might control

The starry pole,

And fallen, fallen light renew!

'O Earth, O Earth, return!

Arise from out the dewy grass!

Night is worn,

And the morn

Rises from the slumbrous mass.

'Turn away no more;

Why wilt thou turn away?

The starry floor,

The watery shore,

Is given thee till the break of day.'

## EARTH'S ANSWER

Earth raised up her head

From the darkness dread and drear,

Her light fled,

Stony, dread,

And her locks covered with grey despair.

'Prisoned on watery shore,

Starry jealousy does keep my den

Cold and hoar;

Weeping o'er,

I hear the father of the ancient men.

'Selfish father of men!

Cruel, jealous, selfish fear!

Can delight,

Chained in night,

The virgins of youth and morning bear.

‘Does spring hide its joy,

When buds and blossoms grow?

Does the sower

Sow by night,

Or the ploughman in darkness plough?

‘Break this heavy chain,

That does freeze my bones around!

Selfish, vain,

Eternal bane,

That free love with bondage bound.'

## THE CLOD AND THE PEBBLE

'Love seeketh not itself to please,

Nor for itself hath any care,

But for another gives its ease,

And builds a heaven in hell's despair.'

So sung a little clod of clay,

Trodden with the cattle's feet,

But a pebble of the brook

Warbled out these metres meet:

'Love seeketh only Self to please,

To bind another to its delight,

Joys in another's loss of ease,

And builds a hell in heaven's despite.'

## HOLY THURSDAY

Is this a holy thing to see

In a rich and fruitful land,—

Babes reduced to misery,

Fed with cold and usurous hand?

Is that trembling cry a song?

Can it be a song of joy?

And so many children poor?

It is a land of poverty!

And their sun does never shine,

And their fields are bleak and bare,

And their ways are filled with thorns,

It is eternal winter there.

For where'er the sun does shine,

And where'er the rain does fall,

Babe can never hunger there,

Nor poverty the mind appal.

## THE LITTLE GIRL LOST

In futurity

I prophesy

That the earth from sleep

(Grave the sentence deep)

Shall arise, and seek

For her Maker meek;

And the desert wild

Become a garden mild.

In the southern clime,

Where the summer's prime

Never fades away,

Lovely Lyca lay.

Seven summers old

Lovely Lyca told.

She had wandered long,

Hearing wild birds' song.

'Sweet sleep, come to me,

Underneath this tree;

Do father, mother, weep?

Where can Lyca sleep?

'Lost in desert wild

Is your little child.

How can Lyca sleep

If her mother weep?

'If her heart does ache,

Then let Lyca wake;

If my mother sleep,

Lyca shall not weep.

'Frowning, frowning night,

O'er this desert bright

Let thy moon arise,

While I close my eyes.'

Sleeping Lyca lay,

While the beasts of prey,

Come from caverns deep,

Viewed the maid asleep.

The kingly lion stood,

And the virgin viewed:

Then he gambolled round

O'er the hallowed ground.

Leopards, tigers, play

Round her as she lay;

While the lion old

Bowed his mane of gold,

And her bosom lick,

And upon her neck,

From his eyes of flame,

Ruby tears there came;

While the lioness

Loosed her slender dress,

And naked they conveyed

To caves the sleeping maid.

## THE LITTLE GIRL FOUND

All the night in woe

Lyca's parents go

Over valleys deep,

While the deserts weep.

Tired and woe-begone,

Hoarse with making moan,

Arm in arm, seven days

They traced the desert ways.

Seven nights they sleep

Among shadows deep,

And dream they see their child

Starved in desert wild.

Pale through pathless ways

The fancied image strays,

Famished, weeping, weak,

With hollow piteous shriek.

Rising from unrest,

The trembling woman pressed

With feet of weary woe;

She could no further go.

In his arms he bore

Her, armed with sorrow sore;

Till before their way

A couching lion lay.

Turning back was vain:

Soon his heavy mane

Bore them to the ground,

Then he stalked around,

Smelling to his prey;

But their fears allay

When he licks their hands,

And silent by them stands.

They look upon his eyes,

Filled with deep surprise;

And wondering behold

A spirit armed in gold.

On his head a crown,

On his shoulders down

Flowed his golden hair.

Gone was all their care.

‘Follow me,’ he said;

‘Weep not for the maid;

In my palace deep,

Lyca lies asleep.’

Then they followèd

Where the vision led,

And saw their sleeping child

Among tigers wild.

To this day they dwell

In a lonely dell,

Nor fear the wolvish howl

Nor the lion's growl.

## THE CHIMNEY-SWEEPER

A little black thing among the snow,

Crying! 'weep! weep!' in notes of woe!

'Where are thy father and mother? Say!'—

'They are both gone up to the church to pray.

'Because I was happy upon the heath,

And smiled among the winter's snow,

They clothed me in the clothes of death,

And taught me to sing the notes of woe.

'And because I am happy and dance and sing,

They think they have done me no injury,

And are gone to praise God and His priest and king,

Who made up a heaven of our misery.'

## NURSE'S SONG

When the voices of children are heard on the green,

And whisperings are in the dale,

The days of my youth rise fresh in my mind,

My face turns green and pale.

Then come home, my children, the sun is gone down,

And the dews of night arise;

Your spring and your day are wasted in play,

And your winter and night in disguise.

## THE SICK ROSE

O rose, thou art sick!

The invisible worm,

That flies in the night,

In the howling storm,

Has found out thy bed

Of crimson joy,

And his dark secret love

Does thy life destroy.

**THE FLY**

Little Fly,

Thy summer's play

My thoughtless hand

Has brushed away.

Am not I

A fly like thee?

Or art not thou

A man like me?

For I dance,

And drink, and sing,

Till some blind hand

Shall brush my wing.

If thought is life

And strength and breath,

And the want

Of thought is death;

Then am I

A happy fly.

If I live,

Or if I die.

## THE ANGEL

I dreamt a dream! What can it mean?

And that I was a maiden Queen

Guarded by an Angel mild:

Witless woe was ne'er beguiled!

And I wept both night and day,

And he wiped my tears away;

And I wept both day and night,

And hid from him my heart's delight.

So he took his wings, and fled;

Then the morn blushed rosy red.

I dried my tears, and armed my fears

With ten thousand shields and spears.

Soon my Angel came again;

I was armed, he came in vain;

For the time of youth was fled,

And grey hairs were on my head.

## THE TIGER

Tiger, tiger, burning bright

In the forests of the night,

What immortal hand or eye

Could frame thy fearful symmetry?

In what distant deeps or skies

Burnt the fire of thine eyes?

On what wings dare he aspire?

What the hand dare seize the fire?

And what shoulder and what art

Could twist the sinews of thy heart?

And, when thy heart began to beat,

What dread hand and what dread feet?

What the hammer? what the chain?

In what furnace was thy brain?

What the anvil? what dread grasp

Dare its deadly terrors clasp?

When the stars threw down their spears,

And watered heaven with their tears,

Did He smile His work to see?

Did He who made the lamb make thee?

Tiger, tiger, burning bright

In the forests of the night,

What immortal hand or eye

Dare frame thy fearful symmetry?

**MY PRETTY ROSE TREE**

A flower was offered to me,

Such a flower as May never bore;

But I said, 'I've a pretty rose tree,'

And I passed the sweet flower o'er.

Then I went to my pretty rose tree,

To tend her by day and by night;

But my rose turned away with jealousy,

And her thorns were my only delight.

## AH, SUNFLOWER

Ah, sunflower, weary of time,

Who countest the steps of the sun;

Seeking after that sweet golden clime

Where the traveller's journey is done;

Where the Youth pined away with desire,

And the pale virgin shrouded in snow,

Arise from their graves, and aspire

Where my Sunflower wishes to go!

## THE LILY

The modest Rose puts forth a thorn,

The humble sheep a threat'ning horn:

While the Lily white shall in love delight,

Nor a thorn nor a threat stain her beauty bright.

## THE GARDEN OF LOVE

I went to the Garden of Love,

And saw what I never had seen;

A Chapel was built in the midst,

Where I used to play on the green.

And the gates of this Chapel were shut,

And 'Thou shalt not' writ over the door;

So I turned to the Garden of Love

That so many sweet flowers bore.

And I saw it was filled with graves,

And tombstones where flowers should be;

And priests in black gowns were walking their rounds,

And binding with briars my joys and desires.

## THE LITTLE VAGABOND

Dear mother, dear mother, the Church is cold;

But the Alehouse is healthy, and pleasant, and warm.

Besides, I can tell where I am used well;

Such usage in heaven will never do well.

But, if at the Church they would give us some ale,

And a pleasant fire our souls to regale,

We'd sing and we'd pray all the livelong day,

Nor ever once wish from the Church to stray.

Then the Parson might preach, and drink, and sing,

And we'd be as happy as birds in the spring;

And modest Dame Lurch, who is always at church,

Would not have bandy children, nor fasting, nor birch.

And God, like a father, rejoicing to see

His children as pleasant and happy as He,

Would have no more quarrel with the Devil or the barrel,

But kiss him, and give him both drink and apparel.

## LONDON

I wander through each chartered street,

Near where the chartered Thames does flow,

A mark in every face I meet,

Marks of weakness, marks of woe.

In every cry of every man,

In every infant's cry of fear,

In every voice, in every ban,

The mind-forged manacles I hear:

How the chimney-sweeper's cry

Every blackening church appals,

And the hapless soldier's sigh

Runs in blood down palace-walls.

But most, through midnight streets I hear

How the youthful harlot's curse

Blasts the new-born infant's tear,

And blights with plagues the marriage hearse.

## THE HUMAN ABSTRACT

Pity would be no more

If we did not make somebody poor,

And Mercy no more could be

If all were as happy as we.

And mutual fear brings Peace,

Till the selfish loves increase;

Then Cruelty knits a snare,

And spreads his baits with care.

He sits down with holy fears,

And waters the ground with tears;

Then Humility takes its root

Underneath his foot.

Soon spreads the dismal shade

Of Mystery over his head,

And the caterpillar and fly

Feed on the Mystery.

And it bears the fruit of Deceit,

Ruddy and sweet to eat,

And the raven his nest has made

In its thickest shade.

The gods of the earth and sea

Sought through nature to find this tree,

But their search was all in vain:

There grows one in the human Brain.

## INFANT SORROW

My mother groaned, my father wept:

Into the dangerous world I leapt,

Helpless, naked, piping loud,

Like a fiend hid in a cloud.

Struggling in my father's hands,

Striving against my swaddling bands,

Bound and weary, I thought best

To sulk upon my mother's breast.

## A POISON TREE

I was angry with my friend:

I told my wrath, my wrath did end.

I was angry with my foe:

I told it not, my wrath did grow.

And I watered it in fears

Night and morning with my tears,

And I sunnèd it with smiles

And with soft deceitful wiles.

And it grew both day and night,

Till it bore an apple bright,

And my foe beheld it shine,

And he knew that it was mine,—

And into my garden stole

When the night had veiled the pole;

In the morning, glad, I see

My foe outstretched beneath the tree.

## A LITTLE BOY LOST

'Nought loves another as itself,
   Nor venerates another so,
Nor is it possible to thought
   A greater than itself to know.

'And, father, how can I love you
   Or any of my brothers more?
I love you like the little bird
   That picks up crumbs around the door.'

The Priest sat by and heard the child;
   In trembling zeal he seized his hair,

He led him by his little coat,
  And all admired his priestly care.
And standing on the altar high,
  'Lo, what a fiend is here!' said he:
'One who sets reason up for judge
  Of our most holy mystery.'
The weeping child could not be heard,
  The weeping parents wept in vain:
They stripped him to his little shirt,
  And bound him in an iron chain,

And burned him in a holy place

Where many had been burned before;

The weeping parents wept in vain.

Are such things done on Albion's shore?

## A LITTLE GIRL LOST

Children of the future age,

Reading this indignant page,

Know that in a former time

Love, sweet love, was thought a crime.

In the age of gold,
Free from winter's cold,
Youth and maiden bright,
To the holy light,
Naked in the sunny beams delight.

Once a youthful pair,
Filled with softest care,
Met in garden bright
Where the holy light
Had just removed the curtains of the night.

There, in rising day,

On the grass they play;

Parents were afar,

Strangers came not near,

And the maiden soon forgot her fear.

Tired with kisses sweet,

They agree to meet

When the silent sleep

Waves o'er heaven's deep,

And the weary tired wanderers weep.

To her father white

Came the maiden bright;

But his loving look,

Like the holy book,

All her tender limbs with terror shook.

Ona, pale and weak,

To thy father speak!

O the trembling fear!

O the dismal care

That shakes the blossoms of my hoary hair!'

## A DIVINE IMAGE

Cruelty has a human heart,

And Jealousy a human face;

Terror the human form divine,

And Secrecy the human dress.

The human dress is forgèd iron,

The human form a fiery forge,

The human face a furnace sealed,

The human heart its hungry gorge.

## A CRADLE SONG

Sleep, sleep, beauty bright,

Dreaming in the joys of night;

Sleep, sleep; in thy sleep

Little sorrows sit and weep.

Sweet babe, in thy face

Soft desires I can trace,

Secret joys and secret smiles,

Little pretty infant wiles.

As thy softest limbs I feel,

Smiles as of the morning steal

O'er thy cheek, and o'er thy breast
Where thy little heart doth rest.
O the cunning wiles that creep
In thy little heart asleep!
When thy little heart doth wake,
Then the dreadful light shall break.

## THE SCHOOLBOY

I love to rise in a summer morn,
When the birds sing on every tree;
The distant huntsman winds his horn,

And the skylark sings with me:

O what sweet company!

But to go to school in a summer morn,—

O it drives all joy away!

Under a cruel eye outworn,

The little ones spend the day

In sighing and dismay.

Ah then at times I drooping sit,

And spend many an anxious hour;

Nor in my book can I take delight,

Nor sit in learning's bower,

Worn through with the dreary shower.

How can the bird that is born for joy

Sit in a cage and sing?

How can a child, when fears annoy,

But droop his tender wing,

And forget his youthful spring!

O father and mother if buds are nipped,

And blossoms blown away;

And if the tender plants are stripped

Of their joy in the springing day,

By sorrow and care's dismay,—

How shall the summer arise in joy,

Or the summer fruits appear?

Or how shall we gather what griefs destroy,

Or bless the mellowing year,

When the blasts of winter appear?

**TO TIRZAH**

Whate'er is born of mortal birth

Must be consumèd with the earth,

To rise from generation free:

Then what have I to do with thee?

The sexes sprung from shame and pride,

Blowed in the morn, in evening died;

But mercy changed death into sleep;

The sexes rose to work and weep.

Thou, mother of my mortal part,

With cruelty didst mould my heart,

And with false self-deceiving tears

Didst blind my nostrils, eyes, and ears,

Didst close my tongue in senseless clay,

And me to mortal life betray.

The death of Jesus set me free:

Then what have I to do with thee?

## THE VOICE OF THE ANCIENT BARD

Youth of delight! come hither

And see the opening morn,

Image of Truth new-born.

Doubt is fled, and clouds of reason,

Dark disputes and artful teazing.

Folly is an endless maze;

Tangled roots perplex her ways;

How many have fallen there!

They stumble all night over bones of the dead;

And feel—they know not what but care;

And wish to lead others, when they should be led.